Houses

An Autobiography

Rhodesia

Ukiyoto Publishing

Dedication

This book is whole-heartedly dedicated to the late Engr. Rodolfo Minguito, and his widow Evelyn Minguito, Rhodesia's parents, who had been pivotal in molding and supporting her, her dreams and aspirations even in the most tumultuous times of her life. It is astonishing how they have pulled their family from the rut and established a brilliant future for their offsprings. Truly, parents are God's instruments for taking care of His beloved children.

By the same token, Rhodesia dedicates this book to her children, Liana and Rodemil, who may be too young today to realize its value. Nevertheless, they may in the near future look back to the history of one of their origins, take pride in their roots, and know how very much loved, desired, and esteemed they are by their mother. It is Rhodesia's deepest wish that they forge their own path, emit their own light, and lead their own blissful and peaceful life.

Lastly, this book is dedicated to all physicians, who have toiled and trained for a long time and even continuously to render the best possible service to their patients, at times uncompensated, but fulfilled for having done a noble deed. This class includes the future physicians, the medical students, who are currently burning midnight oil to peruse over volumes of medical knowledge compiled over centuries. May you perpetuate and even accelerate the revolution of medicine in both affective and technical dimensions.

Above all, this book is humbly dedicated to the Almighty, King of Kings and Lord of Lords, to Him be the glory now and forevermore.

Acknowledgement

Sincerest gratitude is extended to Ms. Janeth Nubla, Rhodesia's best friend, who had assisted and supported her through all her ups and downs, and to Dr. Jazzie Burgos, one of Rhodesia's dearest friends, for introducing her to the publishing company. In this respect, Rhodesia is also indebted to Ukiyoto Publishing for staging a platform where she may be heard and her light may be seen and shared.

The loving support of her sister, Rudilyn, and brother, Rovel are also acknowledged, as are her sisters-in-law, Ate Emi, Iyang, Culing, Aruth, Azon, and mother-in-law, Nanay Sonia. Likewise, the hospital, university, company, and birthing home support during Rhodesia's stay in their setting is highly-appreciated, though the identification of the said domains are deemed better undisclosed by the author.

To all Rhodesia's friends in the academe from the accelerated class batch '90 of M. Hizon Elementary School, Manila Science High School Batch '94, UP Manila BS Biology Block 3, and Pamantasan ng Lungsod ng Maynila Batch 2004, and in the community where they were assigned in Pangasinan, Bulacan and Quezon City, thank you very much. To all the people she had silently loved and taken care of, their memory stays safe in her heart for all her life.

CONTENTS

Prologue

Each entity who avails of the ticket to the greatest adventure called life and traverses it imprints a unique story to the compendium of the history of man. Every person has that story worth telling and listening to, as unique as his face or his fingerprints, a cosmic signature only that person can contribute to the tapestry of life. All experiences, whether blissful or hurting, and the choices he makes towards those experiences, mold a person like how the branches of a tree are molded towards the sun or to gravity. In the end, each person is a masterpiece, whose beauty is too valuable to be silenced to eternity.

This book is the story of Rhodesia, from her birth to the age of 42, when she had the time to pause, look back, and tell her story from a third person point of view. If life begins at 40, then this is only a story of her conception, of the events that molded her into her own unique being, the values those events taught her, and the blessings that came after the lessons. She chose to share this story and not remain silent because perhaps it may cast a light on someone else's path. Perhaps the path may be her own, to evaluate the lessons she has learned before moving forward to the next chapters of her life, or to record her events before they get dimmed down the memory lane.

The chapters are named after the houses she has resided in or passed through indicating significant events in her life. Being in a vocation where their family do not stay in one place but are being assigned to different destinations, she has wandered in many forms of houses. The house, after all, signifies one of the basic needs of man - shelter. It shelters a person and those he holds close to his heart, his family and his belongings. The house also is a fortress from the storm or scorching sun, a place where one can retreat in peace and privacy. It is also a source of comfort, a place of warmth and communions, of laughter and relaxation. One's own house is where he can be his most candid self, where he can cry his heart out, and express his own uniqueness, be it scandinavian or victorian, minimalistic or elaborate. The house thus connotes security, comfort, family, and identity.

A biography is in itself a house. This book is the house of Rhodesia, be her guest and feel at home.

The Slum

Among rows of densely-packed houses constructed in light materials, recycled wooden walls, plastic windows, and iron roofs, there was a shop where jeepneys stopped over to have their tires vulcanized. In the second story of that shop, a starting family squeezed their meager income from the vulcanizing shop to pay their monthly rent. The small room would also accommodate and celebrate the homecoming of a newborn girl, youngest of two, who would be named after one of the countries the father had voyaged to as a seafarer - Rhodesia (*rhodes,* "where roses grow"; *sia,* "victory", "helper"). The baby girl's lullaby had been screeching tires and horns of jeepneys and other vehicles. On the brighter side, she was fully breastfed since they could not afford formula milk, which gave her enough immunity to adapt to the harsh environment where she was planted.

She could not have been born alive if not for the benevolence of the landlady, who shouldered the expense of Cesarean section after the family had been refused in several hospitals due to lack of funds to support the operation. Even in a public hospital, some of the medicines and materials used for the procedure had to be shouldered by the patient's family, or in this case, a benefactor. The family had been so indebted to the kind, old lady who welcomed them in their house and saved the lives of both the mother and the baby girl, but the time came when she had to choose. Her son was released from the jail, and he eyed the vulcanizing shop obsessively for his fresh start. The family had to go find a new home.

Island Hut

The father decided to work again as a seafarer, and had to leave his family to his parents in the province. Aboard the ship on their way to Cebu, rashes appeared on the baby girl's forehead, and spread to her body and extremities, as her temperature spiked. It would still be a day before they landed, and the mother had to patiently wipe her baby with damp cloth to lower the temperature, while continuing breastfeeding. She looked too unwell, with no medicine available. They thought she wouldn't survive, but before they landed, her fever subsided. Her early exposure to a rather harsh environment and the pure breastfeeding boosted her immune system. In a crowded public sea transport, it was fortunate that she did not acquire complications from her measles, like pneumonia or encephalitis.

When they arrived in her grandparents' hut a few meters from the seashore, Rhodesia looked like a fragile thing on the verge of breaking. As days passed, however, she regained strength and turgor she lost from the fever and viral illness. It seemed the sea breeze infused new life in her cells. Her father's salary also infused sustenance to their family, being multiples of 50 when converted to the local currency. However, it also fostered craving on the part of her father's roots.

Being the eldest and most fortunate of the seven children to have landed in a stable job, her father was forced to shoulder the responsibility of supporting his siblings and aging parents. The mother and two toddlers were a nuisance and added expense. In one encounter, the baby girl sustained a wound on her left hand, which bled profusely such that the mother was prompted to defend and protect her offspring. They were subjected to threats that forced them to be adopted by distant relatives, also in the same span of shore. Those relatives wrote the father about the harsh treatment to his family, so he decided to let them return to Manila.

Own Home

Lola Betty, grandmother on the maternal side, bought for them a piece of land where a dilapidated house stood, and they could pay the cost at their own due time. They could only afford minimal repair so they stayed in the half-wrecked house they could call their own. Papa Rudy planted around the house, which not too long grew into trees and shrubs, and made the environment a very pleasing garden though still situated in the heart of Tondo, Manila, near the pier where cargo and passenger ships dock. Rhodesia used to climb up their rusty roof and sit there watching the magnificence of those ships, the sea, and the setting sun.

Their "own home" was a corner in the perimeter of a basketball court, where children go out in the afternoon, run like wild horses, and laugh their hearts out, and Rhodesia was not an exception; she had her own share of child's play. There was a barangay hall on the opposite corner, where a group of Hindu teachers conducted an outreach program for preschoolers. Rhodesia was two years old then, and was schooled by kind, tall men with equally tall aquiline noses and deep-set eyes, and dressed in orange flowing robes and turban wrapped on the crown of their head. They taught her how to pray in the lotus position, and how to appose the palms in front of the forehead then sternum and bow to greet.

During recess, Rhodesia would just cross the basketball court to have her snack, then still breastfeeding. She was three when she recited the first poem she made,

> *"Mahal kita Nanay ,*
>
> (I love you mother)
>
> *Di kita iiwan,*
>
> (I will not leave you)
>
> *Wag mo kong iwanan,*
>
> (Please don't leave me too)
>
> *Mahal kita Nanay."*
>
> (I love you mother).

Come graduation ceremonies staged also on the basketball court, Rhodesia received several honors from the kind tall men who served as her light during her tender formative years. She was valedictorian for two consecutive years, and delivered her speech to her fellow children and their parents at the age of four. Her father's heart swelled at that time, having gone up the stage several times to put on her ribbon or medal, alternating with her mom and her Lola Betty. Few months after that, her father mustered the courage to take and fortunately passed a series of examinations which furthered his rank as a seafarer, from 3rd to 2nd to 1st to chief marine engineer, and with that, their fortune also boosted. They were able to pay their *own home* in full.

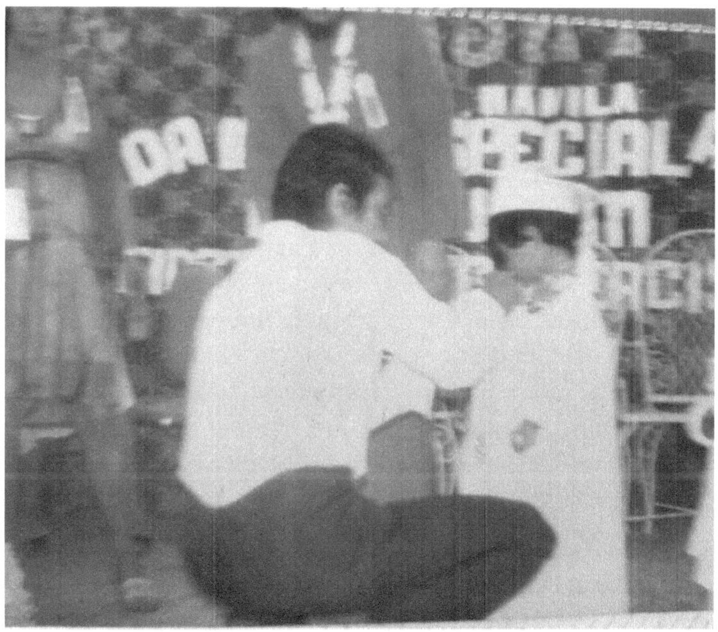

The Two-Storey Concrete Own Home

In time, the family peeled the wrecked house like a shell, and built a two-storey concrete house. The mother dressed up the house elaborately, and made sure the sofas were big and soft and comfortable, as well as the beds. They enjoyed having rare technology at that time such as television, and they had a veranda where they could safely watch the happenings in the basketball court.

Rhodesia was admitted to primary school at five years old, conditionally after having passed an entrance examination. She did not give them a chance to doubt, however, as she won her first inter-school competition on poetry writing at the age of five. After three years, she was valedictorian of primary school and nominated to take an exam for acceleration to intermediate school. She fortunately passed and skipped a grade, but had to transfer to a school where the special education class was conducted. In that school, she was again representative to various quiz bees and graduated valedictorian.

Her father was all the more inspired to go home every summer to pin medals and accept trophies. On one occasion when Rhodesia was nine years old, her father was also on cloud nine while sitting beside the city mayor, as her little girl delivered her speech during the launching of her book, *Nature and Child's Life Experiences*, an anthology of poems. She was then hailed as the Youngest Book Author of the Philippines, and the book was approved to be a reference book for 4th grade, the grade she skipped.

Blessings came like succeeding waves, as she became one of Ten Outstanding Filipino Child Achievers for Academic Excellence, and the City of Manila recognized her contribution to school journalism as an Outstanding Manilan in the 421st *Araw ng Maynila* (Manila Day). The poor, young, and frail girl from the slums stood among the most distinguished men and women of the City of Manila, whose silver hairs crown their heads with wisdom and benefaction. Beyond the academe, she was featured in several TV shows as the little girl from the slums teaching a group of out-of-school youths within her reach.

(Rhodesia, 4th from right)

The Three-Storey Home With Roof Deck Garden

The once lush garden was converted to a parking space, and the second floor extended above that. Rhodesia's room was placed on the third floor, with a spacious sala outside housing her paintings, a library, and a guest room. Ascending a flight of stairs, the garden was transferred to the roof deck, where a covered swing and outdoor sala set were beautifully positioned. Rhodesia still climbed to the roof, though now not anymore rusty but comfortably elegant, to enjoy the tranquility and humility of the setting sun on the sea, and the ships coming to and from the harbor.

She has had her own share of medieval period. After four years of rigorous training in Manila Science High School, Rhodesia became a free-spirited BS Biology student in the University of the Philippines-Manila. She yearned for a different kind of wisdom, and shunned expectations. She worked as a student assistant in the Department of Physical Sciences and Mathematics, and filed a leave of absence to do some soul-searching. Even then, she was active in Pahinungod programs, such as medical missions in far-flung provinces, streetkids program, and emergency room and Cancer Institute hospice care programs. In the church, she handled and spearheaded preschool and out-of-school youth and adult education in Baseco Island. She enjoyed riding a boat to the island, where her students were waiting eagerly for her each weekday. She felt sad when there was even one missing, and walked the shorelines to visit the absentee. She was amazed how people who could hardly even read, could deliver hypotheses on scientific concepts she posed. She brought the students out of the island to the National Museum as a field trip, and hoped that somehow they would carry that light in their hearts and perpetuate it to others.

Rhodesia's Out-of-School Youth Students

from Baseco Island to the National Museum

She was a bit delayed when she returned to the academe, but still topped the National Medical Admission Test, and was nominated for best thesis for a study she and her partner conducted in the Marine Science Institute in UP Diliman. She took the Doctor of Medicine program in *Pamantasan ng Lungsod ng Maynila* (University of the City of Manila) as a full scholar. Situated in Intramuros, she enjoyed the serenity, richness of history, and cultural heritage of the setting. She fell in love with the place, and fell in love while in the place.

(Rhodesia, center, 2nd row from front)

The spacious sala on the third floor was where they finalized their goodbyes. She cooked for him his favorite meal for their last supper together. She just came back to Manila from their vacation villa in Bohol, a tactic used by her mother to separate them. Before she left, they spent a wonderful walk along the cobbled pavements of Intramuros, visited Jose Rizal's simulated dungeon near the river, and raced stepping on the late national hero's footprints. As she was praying with her head bowed on his shoulder while they were sitting on a bench facing the river, a group of Japanese tourists passed by and asked if he made her cry. They seemed to foretell because while she was away, he was transferred destination, and had contemplated how continuing their relationship could potentially ruin her career, and how the relationship was not blessed by the parents. In the card he once gave her, he wrote, "Smile when you think of me". In a letter she gave him after the break-up, she wrote, "We do not always marry the ones we love; we do not always love the ones we marry," a bitter pill she had to swallow someday. The separation almost cost her the scholarship and her academic ranking, as she just managed to go through each day, missed responsibilities, and almost could not read her tear-soaked exam questionnaires. It seemed her light dimmed out.

The Mansion

It was the largest, most extravagant house she had ever seen, like ones she could only see in movies and paintings. Two winding flights of stairs converge on a colossal veranda, and the whole house seemed to glimmer with dazzling lights even after sundown. Rhodesia was fetched from the hospital with one of her patient's private vehicles to deliver a short talk for a thanksgiving ceremony. As she hopped in the car, she was surprised that a gift was waiting for her - a set of books which she read repeatedly and loved, and a Marks & Spencer necklace with a brown circular pendant. It was a pleasant surprise, but the immensity of their mansion surprised her even more.

"I was working the night shift in the emergency room; she was endorsed to me as a case of migraine headache, and was given medication intramuscularly. According to the endorsement, she drove herself to the ER after lunch, complaining of a severe headache, and after giving the medication, she was just sleeping and they were waiting for her to wake up to be discharged (sent home). When I did a physical examination on the patient, she had involuntarily urinated, comatose, and had anisocoric (unequal size) pupils. I scanned her phone to contact any relative, and luckily I was able to talk to her best friend who contacted her family. They promptly came, and I explained we needed to do a CT scan, which confirmed my suspicion - she had a large intracranial hemorrhage. The patient was aptly transferred to St. Luke's Medical Center where she was operated on, and thank God she's with us today." The patient was a very beautiful young lass taking Interior Design in Singapore, and just came home for vacation; it could have been a great loss to her loved ones and family and to the world to not see such angelic face again.

The emergency room had been Rhodesia's home for twelve years, managing and saving patients with near-fatal asthma, myocardial infarction (heart attack), stroke, malignant hypertension, pneumonia, drowning, electrocution, vehicular accidents, dengue fever, diarrhea, gunshot wounds, lacerations, acute appendicitis, foreign body in a child's nose or ears, parturition (childbirth), and the list was endless. Twice a week, she handled medical biochemistry classes in her alma mater for two years as a compensated payback for being their scholar. It had been a busy, useful, and beautiful life to serve the sick and suffering and save lives, and the countless sleepless nights she spent in the hospital seemed to pass like a breeze.

Also in this setting, one of her suitors used to stay outside the emergency room overnight while she was on duty, and supply breakfast for all the ER team including the nurses, nursing aids, and guard. He had been so good to her but on a dinner beside the bay, she confessed that she had no feelings for him. He was working overseas and came to the Philippines just to court her in person, so he just had to return to where he was working. However, while they were dining, a little girl approached to sell a white rose, which he still bought and gave her. When he was already overseas, he received her message that the white rose was her sign and that she was accepting his love. When he returned to the Philippines, he already got her a diamond ring which she accepted. It was because of him that her eyes were freed from thick glasses and contact lenses by sponsoring and taking care of her during her eye surgery. For all that, there came a time when they really had to part, she returned the diamond ring but never any of his calls or messages. Albeit too late, she learned from a teacher not to impose our sign to God, but wait for His sign to us.

The Palace

One night during Rhodesia's duty in the emergency room, the senior house officer received a call and gave her instructions that a service vehicle will pick her up to attend to a patient. Emergency kit was prepared and she followed as ordered. They passed through what looked like walls but suddenly opened like a maze, and even after serving there for quite some time, she still could not figure out how to reach the place. When she arrived, she found a pale, gasping man in his twilight years. A medical team surrounded him, and assisted her in intubation (putting a tube to the patient's trachea through the mouth to assist breathing) which was successful, the ambubag was placed on the tube and pumped, and the patient's oxygenation improved, while the gasping subsided.

When she looked around after the procedure was done, she realized she was surrounded by the family and she thought she must have been in another world because their beauty was ethereal. When she looked back at the patient, now pink and composed, she realized she just saved the life of "the king". They allowed her to be included in the medical team, took care of the king, healed all his wounds from being confined in bed, as he grew stronger, while the kingdom unknowingly rejoiced and celebrated another anniversary. However, one National Heroes' Day afternoon when she was off-duty, she received a call that the king had passed away. When the news was announced, the whole kingdom wailed in mourning, and many citizens also died due to severe grief.

The wake and burial of the king was solemn, orderly, and dignified, but even in silence, the grief and sorrow of everyone was palpable. As Rhodesia sat among the medical team, whom the family had considered their extended kin, she reminisced how she would enter his room at night to monitor and see him glowing, how she patiently dressed and treated all his wounds until all were healed, how she would open the curtains in the morning to let the morning sunshine in, play his favorite music, and read him the newspaper so he'll know what's happening outside the palace. Hardly holding back her own tears, she mused, "If God will also take my life now, I consider it fulfilled and well-lived; it was a great honor to serve and take care of the king in his last days."

The Townhouse

True to her forecast, Rhodesia wed out of faith and duty. When she was young, she had already plotted that she would get settled at the age of 27, and prayed at that time for her companion for life. As if divinely orchestrated, someone came who swept her parents off their feet, and she conceded with the faith that the union was blessed by her parents. The wedding was extravagant, held in a newly-renovated historical church, with all-male chorale singing like archangels, and a reception in a five-star equally historic hotel. Her students graced her celebration with their celestial rendition of *"The Prayer,"* while nephews perfused the atmosphere with saxophone and piano melodies. The man was a responsible husband and amply able to raise and take care of a family, and they resided in a two-storey townhouse type housing accommodation. It was a beautiful house, the walls were colored green, with a spacious sala, six-seater dining table, and one large and one small bedroom, albeit too much for a starting family, until they were blessed with a bouncing baby girl with an angelic face.

When Rhodesia's beloved elder sister Rudilyn got operated on from her brain tumor, Rhodesia took care of her when she was admitted in the hospital. Rudilyn was conceiving her fourth child when she experienced nausea, vomiting, headaches, and dizziness which seemed part of her pregnancy, but when she had episodes of amaurosis fugax, or times of temporary blindness, they sought ophthalmology consult, and when a fundoscopy was done, there was papilledema, which was a sign of increased pressure in the brain. Rudilyn underwent cranial CT scan, and true enough, a big tumor was seen on the posterior fossa, the part of the brain where structures that govern balance, vision, and even breathing, were located. The tumor had to be removed, or else it might compress the breathing center of the brain and she would die, but anesthesia during the operation would harm the baby. They decided to postpone the operation, with close monitoring and possible emergency operation of her brain tumor if condition worsened. With the grace of God, Rudilyn was still able to give birth to her baby girl, and underwent operation of brain tumor after 3 months. The other patients in her room where she was admitted and whom she already established friendship with, had complications during their brain operation, most died, but Rhodesia still pushed through with the operation. It was a damned-if-you-do, damned-if-you-don't decision. With God's infinite grace once again, Rudilyn survived the operation, and her sister was always beside her. However, one time Rhodesia felt dizzy and almost passed out on her way to the hospital. She thought it was just overfatigue, but it seemed God never ran out of blessings and surprises, she tested positive in the pregnancy test.

The wonder of kindling a new life in her bosom enchanted her, despite the severity of her morning sickness in the first trimester. She vomited every after food intake, and felt weak, drained, and dried. There was subchorionic hemorrhage in ultrasound, showing partial detachment of the budding baby from the walls of the uterus, as she noted spotting of blood from her undergarments, which worsened to moderate bleeding. She needed complete bed rest, and was admitted for IV tocolysis (administration directly to bloodstream of medicine that will delay passing out of embryo or fetus). There was a significant possibility that she might lose her baby, but typical of Rhodesia's spirit, she held on to the new life she was carrying. They passed the afflictions, the baby held on too, and Rhodesia was again performing her duties in the emergency room even when her bump was visible at seven months. She was on duty in the emergency room when her bag of waters leaked, and was admitted for induction of labor.

Unlike Rhodesia's rocky beginnings, her baby girl Liana was born via normal spontaneous delivery under epidural anesthesia ("painless labor"), and since Rhodesia was working in the hospital, they shouldered minimal cost which would just be deducted from her salary. Liana was less than a year old when Rhodesia served the king, and she was still breastfeeding her then. When Liana was three years old, she was able to play pick-up lines with her grandfather Papa Rudy who stayed with them for a few weeks after getting discharged from the hospital. He had already survived a heart attack overseas and retired in the paradise he set up in Bohol, but had to come to Manila to be treated due to worsening difficulty of breathing. He was diagnosed with leukemia, and Rhodesia watched over him in the hospital while conducting her duty in the evenings, and preparing documents for setting up a medical school in the morning.

Papa Rudy decided to go home to spend time with Nanay Eve in the home they toiled for and built, the first one they called their own. He had been admitted several times for blood transfusions, until one day, Rhodesia's sister referred to her that there was something strange about their Papa, that he seemed to be sitting and then reclining repeatedly. She told them to bring him to the nearest hospital, as he seemed uneasy. Papa Rudy was brought to the hospital where Rhodesia had her junior internship, but it was already full at that time. When the resident doctor saw the surname, he repeated it, which reminded him of his biochemistry teacher as a freshman medical student. Nanay Eve confirmed that Rhodesia taught and also was trained in that medical school system. Papa Rudy was overjoyed to hear his daughter called Dra. Minguito again, after getting married and using a different surname. The resident doctor contacted Rhodesia and explained that they set up a special room for her Papa in the emergency room, and that he was undergoing full diagnostic work-up. Rhodesia confirmed that she was on her way to the hospital though it was quite far. They were quite surprised that after the X-ray, Papa Rudy just peacefully slept in his stretcher, pulseless and breathless. When Rhodesia came, they had done resuscitation for almost an hour, and she allowed them to cease the futile efforts. He rested successful, bountiful, and fulfilled.

The High-Rise

In the terrace of a two-bedroom unit on the 6th floor of a condominium, Rhodesia and Liana and the newborn baby boy could feel the cool breeze as they watched the two other towering buildings surrounding a central giant pool. She prayed fervently for a baby boy, knowing it was her duty to continue her husband's surname being the only boy in their family, and in less than a year, her gift was delivered, again without any complication in pregnancy and parturition. The baby boy was sturdy, highly mobile, energetic, and handsome. However, she fully took care of him for only two weeks, and was able to sustain breastfeeding for only six months. Her duties as the founding college secretary of a new college of medicine extracted her from home.

The task was daunting, another mission that just fell on her lap. At 32, they say she was the youngest college secretary of a college of medicine, but titles never enthralled her. For her, it was just a mission to be accomplished. The time they applied for a permit to operate, the Commission on Higher Education (CHED) was pushing for a moratorium, that was, no more new medical schools to be founded. Two times the dean had to be replaced because they could not meet the commission's stringent standards, but she remained as the college secretary doing the necessary documentary, administrative, and academic tasks to establish the college. The commission required a transformative medical curriculum, and the college academic council spearheaded by the director, dean, and college secretary developed a remarkable curriculum with a medical humanities course series to imbibe empathy and compassion as medical professionals, an excellent imaging course series that arm the students with skills in interpreting radiographs, ultrasound, CT scan and MRI, and an innovative community medicine course series to expose and hone their hearts to service to humanity. Rhodesia never cowered despite difficulties and obstacles, and with support and cooperation from the top management, university, college academic council, and the staff of the college, the College of Medicine received its permit to operate, and was recognized by the CHED to produce future physicians.

Sometimes when Rhodesia traveled, she noticed that an educational institution laid down the social architecture of the place. In a town offering a bachelor of law, there were legal offices around the town. The sweetest fruit in Rhodesia's labor were her students - they were so brilliant, enthusiastic, and promising, like a very fertile land where to plant and mold into compassionate physicians who will also love and serve their patients like their own kin, while being the best and excellent medical strategist in diagnosis and treatment. She strived to keep the college clean and orderly, and uprooted weeds which may harm the good crops. After all, a human being, no matter the status in life, deserves the best care from a physician, and she hoped she had helped ignite a light that would continue to the future generations of physicians. Her mission was accomplished, it was time to move on and continue her journey.

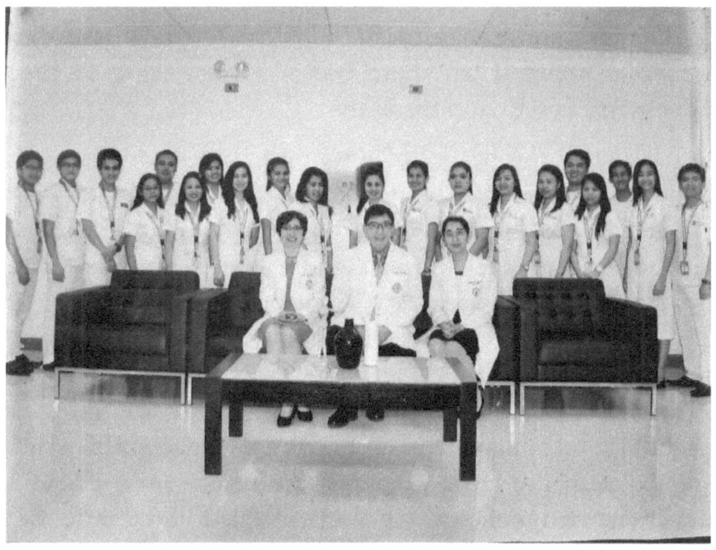

Pioneers - The Dean, Director, Rhodesia (front row, rightmost) and the students

The Rural Antique House

When Rhodesia's family was assigned in Pangasinan, they were told the house was too old and would be condemned soon; but when she first stepped into the house, she deeply adored the place. The house was a two-storey building, made of solid wood, the kind of wood that was abundant during the olden times when forests were still lush and teeming with life. There were three colossal bedrooms on the second story, with king-sized beds, antique wooden dressers and cabinets. Outside the three bedrooms was a sala, where Rhodesia placed the bookshelf, her portrait in white coat, and a rocking chair matching the antique sala set. This would be her and her children's placid place. On the ground floor were a sala furnished with a modern sofa, where a lot of visitors were received, her husband's office, a dining area with a circular wooden dining table, a kitchen, and a bathroom. The elders said that "the king" stayed in this house when there was a special event in the place, hence the grand design and furniture.

Time has dulled the beauty of the house, but Rhodesia recognized its grandeur. She did not waste time but repainted the walls with white and bordered with light turquoise, placed a chandelier and green carpet on the receiving hall, and a large painting of a tranquil forest with calmly flowing low waterfalls. She repainted all the furniture and cabinets with coffee brown paint and lacquer, and polished the floor to sparkle. She planted red roses in the backyard. Soon, the old, soon-to-be-condemned antique house was a revived heritage house, teeming with visitors from all walks of life who loved and laughed with the family. There were three senior citizen sisters who never married, children who sat on the sofa to watch TV and play with her kids after worship service, school principals and teachers, dean of university, farmers, hog raisers, and pretty lasses who went straight to their heritage home after coming from their nearby university. It was as if the antique house had a light that delighted the community and soon turned friends of the family.

Rhodesia's medical service continued when needed. In one of their previous destinations in that area, she met one of the pioneer pastors, then 96 years of age, with dimming memory except for the doctrines engraved in his heart. One day after coming from the movie theater with her children, the retired pastor's daughter approached her and said that they had already prayed for his father who was so weak, and with difficulty of breathing but refused to go to the hospital. She heard crackles from auscultation of his lungs, and at his age, it was high-risk for him to develop such infections. She maximized oral medications to combat infection, as well as establish hydration even without an intravenous line. With God's grace, he survived. When the family returned there again after the New Year celebration, they learned that the retired pastor slipped and had a laceration on his scalp, which Rhodesia patiently cleaned and dressed everyday until healed. Fortunately, his sensorium had not changed, and there was no limitation of motion or weakness on either side of his body, until the family's destination was again transferred to the antique house. Several months later, she received a message from his daughter thanking her for taking care of her father while she was with them, and that his father's spirit had finally joined the Creator.

The Bunkhouse

Due to lockdowns during the COVID-19 pandemic, Rhodesia's family stayed in one of the bunkhouses provided by the company where she was serving as a medical consultant. It was a small but orderly house made of customized steel like a container van, with a four-seater dining table, a comfortable sofa bed, a console with flat screen TV, a refrigerator, a comfort room with hot shower, sink and utensils, and a double deck bed with pull-out accommodating four persons to rest. There were hundreds of those bunkhouses, comfortably spaced, which was ideal in mitigating spread of the coronavirus.

The clinic was situated on the entrance to a garden Rhodesia loved to roam frequently while it was closed to visitors during the lockdown. She traced a succession of giant hearts stuffed with leaves and flowers overarching the path, then entered the aviary to spend soothing moments with the serenading birds in various forms, sizes and colors. Afterwards, she would pass through a tunnel of arch-shaped lights, and hanging violets, and enter an air-conditioned dome with carpeted lawn and petunias in bloom. She would then descend a flight of green stairs facing giant peacock-shaped foliage, and at the right three equally enormous waterfall-shaped greeneries, and at the left, a simulation of Noah's arc, with roaming camels and donkeys. She would enter the jungle-inspired butterfly garden, and watched how greedy, icky caterpillars metamorphosed to mesmerizing beauty after brief moments of slumber in their cocoons. She would then roam the vast garden, with plants shaped like the three blind mice, and a giant bear with a big heart, and towering superheroes like superman, wonder woman, kung fu panda, aquaman, and ironman posed for action. She would pass through a hanging bridge and clink coins on the railings to enjoy the swarming kois, and watch a black swan serenely floating on the pond, poised like royalty. She would go beyond a curtain of hanging vines, and spend the rest of her reveries on a red bridge in a tranquil Japanese garden with pink flowers, sculptured rocks and bonsai, and little white stones surrounding a wooden hut.

When the world was grappling for a formula to combat the coronavirus, Rhodesia instituted antigen testing for periodic screening of company employees, quarantine and isolation, contact tracing, and vaccination. PCR was too expensive, there was a delay in release of results, and even the recovered may still turn out a positive result because of remnant nucleic acids, and antibody testing was inferential as to who really was infected at the moment. She and a nurse tested thousands of employees in different locations, isolated the sick, traced and tested contacts, and managed the mild to moderate cases until they were fully well. With God's grace, they were able to admit almost eight hundred patients, and everyone returned to work recuperated.

One of the patients, a sixty-six year old dress-maker in the garments section, was more gravely afflicted, her oxygen saturation was falling even with oxygen support. In one of Rhodesia's visits to her bunkhouse, she was holding her hand, teary-eyed, she said, "*Doktora, simula po ng bata ako, di pa po ako nachecheck-up* (Ever since I was a child, I haven't seen a doctor)." It was a priceless token of appreciation, much like the church offering of the last penny from a poor widow. At a time of strict social distancing, Rhodesia never shied away from the afflicted, and families appreciated her genuine care and interaction with them when others, even their closest relatives, detached from them. The patient survived, among others like her case, and was able to return to work.

Few months before the pandemic, Rhodesia was also assigned to revive a birthing home. Wary of the paucity of her knowledge and expertise, she took up a Master's Degree in Hospital Administration, which she was able to complete during the pandemic while doing her administrative and clinical duties. With support from the top management, all requirements in infrastructure (clinic design), equipment, manpower, and protocols were accomplished, and the center was given license to operate by the Department of Health. She was able to unite the team in weekly prayers, gatherings, and lectures, and trained the nurses and midwives as required, and to uphold a high quality of service. When the pandemic afflicted the country, the birthing home became a sanctuary for mothers who were afraid to go to the hospital because all hospitals then were brimming with COVID patients, some even given oxygen support in their own cars only. The mothers and babies were well taken care of, tested for COVID prior to admission, given prescribed vaccinations, and tested for inborn errors of metabolism despite the chaos of the pandemic.

(Rhodesia, 3rd from right, MHA Graduation)

Even after close encounters and exposure to all spectrum of patients, from asymptomatic, mild, moderate, to severe cases, Rhodesia and her kids never contracted the disease or tested positive in routine antigen and PCR testing. Nonetheless, it was said that we meet people and go places for a reason, and a season. When vaccines became widely available to the vulnerable population and the company workers, Rhodesia's mission in that locality was also concluded.

The Executive Houses

The ravages of the COVID-19 pandemic did not spare the untouchables, even the royalty, the presidents of powerful nations, and the upper echelons of society. The etiologic agent SARS-CoV2 proved its crown being a *coronavirus* was even more powerful than theirs. No amount of money or power made them immune to a novel disease that baffled the best and brightest in the medical field worldwide. Those physicians, nurses, and other frontliners succumbed to the disease along with their patients, even their lives were claimed, among almost seven million spirits around the world freed from their perished remains.

Rhodesia was sent to attend to a powerful man, though out of her league or her current scope of duties. She entered a marble pathway to a solid oak door and broad cushioned L-shaped sofa, to polished wooden stairs, to his room where he was groaning due to fever, devitalizing cough, shortness of breath, and general body malaise. Rhodesia initiated treatment while preparing patient transfer to a hospital because he was on the verge of deteriorating fast based on his symptoms, body habitus, and comorbid conditions. The emergency room in a private hospital was overflowing, but Rhodesia negotiated, persisted, and pulled some strings so her patient may be given the chance to be admitted. They stayed in the ambulance at the parking lot for quite some time while having some diagnostic work-ups done, then in the emergency room for another day, before getting admitted to a private room in the COVID ward. Rhodesia took turns with her team in being the patient attendant, and voiced her opinion that even after three days of treatment the patient was not improving. The hospital personnel were very responsive, did a repeat CT scan of the chest, and upon seeing that the lung infiltrates were indeed extending, stepped up the treament regimen. Meanwhile, his wife at home also developed diarrhea, fever and cough, and Rhodesia sent her oral medicines and instructions. The powerful man who thought he was joining his colleagues who already passed away due to COVID-19 joined instead his wife in joyful celebration of their union and recovery.

In another mission, Rhodesia had been visiting a household in an exclusive village weekly to ensure their family and helpers were COVID-free by both antigen and antibody testing. One of those visits was rushed, since the lady of the house was excited because at last she was given the permission and freedom to attend to her burgeoning responsibilities in various places. A couple of weeks later, during the routine visit, she was symptomatic and tested positive, and not too long, her husband also developed symptoms and had the same result. They were confined in one of their houses, and attended by the best medical personnel, with avant-garde treatment and intensive care set-up. Rhodesia was called again when one by one the medical personnel were being pulled out because they also tested positive and needed treatment and recuperation. She loved how their roof allowed the natural light to enter their sala facing the library, where she spent lee hours perusing some of the books; but when she entered their room, her heart breaks seeing this family she had loved and protected now bed-ridden. The lady of the house once told her, *"Alam mo doktora, maganda yang ginagawa mo, iba pa rin may human touch (You know what doctor, what you are doing is good, human touch is still different.),"* when she soothed her with essential oils to boost her endorphins, and facilitate lymphatic drainage of her edema, at a time when all medical personnel were covered with personal protective equipment from head to toe.

Unfortunately, Rhodesia learned that at the bunkhouse, her husband was also deteriorating from COVID so she had to go home at sundown to attend to him. A couple of days afterwards, when her husband was already recovering, she resumed her morning duties in the executive house. Woefully, the mighty man of the house had been deteriorating since midnight, with his blood pressure unstable despite maximum inotropes and vasopressors (medicines to increase the force of heart pumping and maintain blood pressure), and he passed away that day despite hours of resuscitation. His wife was transferred to the hospital but joined him exactly a week after, and they were buried in one marble tomb. Through their example, Rhodesia's dream was transformed from being a dutiful, faithful servant, to spending eternal repose with someone she truly loves - *to have and to hold, in sickness and in health, till death do them part.*

The Loft

During her stay in the company, she knew from experience the impermanence of all things. She wanted to have something to remind her of her service in that season, so she invested in a house in a pleasant and peaceful village beside a road leading to the expressway. The house welcomed the sunrise each day, had a parking space with chocolate brown metal gates, a small garden on the side, a cozy living and dining area with wood-style granite tiles, six-seater glass dining table, library of her beloved books, a smart TV installed on a wall, and posted pictures of her children when they graduated from elementary and preschool. There was a small kitchen, bathroom, and stairs leading to the loft where a single bed and air-conditioning unit were installed to cool the entire house. On the white-dove colored wall opposite the bed was a wall paper of foliage and butterflies, and the words ``Beautiful Life'' in calligraphic font. On the far wall across the loft, Rhodesia placed her self-portraits when she graduated from college, when she was in her white coat, and when she was in a Filipiniana gown during her latest graduation ceremony. Rhodesia called this house her *Sacred Space*.

In her unquenchable thirst for wisdom, Rhodesia used the pandemic season not only in service and administration, but also in learning. She learned from the people manning the birthing home, the drivers and cleaners, the top management, the patients, published studies, mass media, and the authorities. She proactively searched and finished forty courses in Mindvalley, an educational platform offering deep wisdom and guidance to living an extraordinary life, and also took technical courses in Coursera, OpenWHO, Medscape, MIMS, and Biotecnika. She willed to allocate her earnings and her time on worthwhile investments. Even after all these continuing personal and professional development and education, Rhodesia still felt like a blank slate waiting to be written on.

The White Houses Of The Highlands

Rhodesia's husband was the fourth and only boy of six children. When he had to depart for a long time to fulfill his assignments, he would leave them to his mother and sisters for safety and security. They also started poor, but with the grace of God, all of his sisters except the one who had meningitis during childhood, graduated with flying colors. They settled in an area of the Sierra Madre mountains called Pantabangan. When all of them married, they erected their houses in the same vast land, all white and distinctive in architecture. At the foot of their family village was their rustic restaurant called *"Hillocks"*, followed by the house of the firstborn reminiscent of classic American mountain lodge after ascending a small bridge with creeping vines, and low stairs. Ascending further was the house of the second sister which was a white Scandinavian bungalow, followed by the house of the fourth sister which was a colossal white bungalow surrounded with large glass windows, where their mother and third sister who was developmentally delayed due to childhood brain infection also resided. Near the top of their parcel of mountain was the house of the youngest, a modern, two-storey white house with a veranda overlooking the relaxing Pantabangan Dam and mountain view. All of them had children of their own, and the compound was a village in itself, a perfect example of extended family but with the privacy of their own houses in one sizable land. This was where Rhodesia and her family retreated for one week per year in her fifteen years of marriage.

The Hillocks

During one of their stay in one of the white houses, the husband of the firstborn accidentally cut his finger on the wheels of the deep well motor. Rhodesia was having a meeting then with the medical officers of Pantabangan to help them in setting-up their infirmary. When Rhodesia came home, the injured was already in the hospital, and returned home with staples on his fingers hoping that the nearly avulsed part may heal and connect with the hand. Rhodesia cleaned and treated the wound for a month, and helped return its functionality for him to be able to help run errands in their restaurant. She also took care of wide abrasions on a nephew's leg, arms and hands after a motorcycle accident, and monitored the blood pressure of anyone in the family seeking her care.

One night, a niece who was pregnant and expecting noted random contractions and her pads continuously wet with watery material. At night she consulted Rhodesia to ask casually, though she was not troubled because she had high tolerance to pain, and she was scheduled for follow-up after two more weeks. Rhodesia explained that she had to be admitted because the amniotic fluid that suspends the baby and was her source of nutrients and oxygen was already leaking indicating that her membrane had already ruptured. Possible complication if the condition was not diagnosed early enough was that the baby may acquire infection, or the fluid may be too scanty to support oxygenation and nutrient delivery and cause distress to the fetus. When she was admitted to the hospital, she underwent an emergency cesarean section and her baby matured in an incubator.

Before Rhodesia and her children left from Pantabangan, they celebrated the homecoming of the newest member of their extended family.

The House Of Worship

Rhodesia resided in many other houses and served people from all walks of life - pregnant, babies, elderly, productive age, underprivileged, affluent, disabled physically, emotionally, or mentally, the list again was endless. No matter how many places she had been, she considered the house of worship as her only home. It was there where she found solace, serenity, and boundless love, and in her heart was encrypted, "The Lord is my inheritance," the dictum of the Levites who didn't have any land they could call their own in order to serve in the house of the Lord. As she silently sat on a corner of her Father's house, her heart mused -

God, thank you for snatching me from death several times in my life. Thank you for the experiences, lessons, and overwhelming blessings of life, good health, a sound mind, purpose, family, friends, and the right and freedom to worship and connect with You. Thank you for giving me the chance to perpetuate all these in the people that I can reach and touch, and thank you for allowing them to also teach and impart to me. Thank you for where I am now, where I have been, and where I will ever be.

I am here, my God, I am Yours, make me an instrument of Thy peace and goodness. My past, present and future belongs to You. I have done trespasses, please forgive me, and forge my heart to be molded according to Your divine design. I hope that everything I do may bring glory to Your holy name. I am Thy servant, Thy will be done. In the name of the Lord Jesus Christ, Amen.

The Suburban Villa

It was a simple home, appropriate in proportion for a family with two kids - a teen daughter, and a first-grader boy. It had a garden with violets, enough parking space, wide kitchen, a stretch for both living and dining rooms so that the television can be enjoyed even when eating, a bathroom, and two bedrooms. The best part of the house was outside, the great expanse of blue skies with white fluffy clouds like the wings of angels above, and the green meadows and trees below. No towering buildings or crowded houses blocked the view. It was a breath-taking countryside scenery, serene but full of life, accentuated by the sweet songs of birds and flutter of white butterflies.

Rhodesia now rendered the time and passion snatched by her years of service to her daughter and son, and maintaining a warm, loving environment where they can thrive and grow and choose their own lifepath. Liana was now tall at fourteen, with a pretty face, wide forehead, and long straight black hair, atop broad shoulders and lean body. She was a courageous young lass, with resolute will, responsible, quiet and spent time mostly in her room with background music, and independently able to solve mishaps that happen in the house when left alone. Rodemil was now vibrant at six, active, energetic, loved to dance in time with the beat, had the maximum 200 friends in Roblox, protective of loved ones, fashionable, and digested his math lessons like a piece of cake. The lessons and training Rhodesia had gathered in her lifetime now guided her little ones, but they had their own story to craft, their own choices to make. She could only shower them love and support, while praying their path led them to blessedness and peace.

At the roof of her life, Rhodesia was still watching the magnificence of her own sun humbly bowing before the sea, hoping that with the last rays she may cast, some plants may still be showered with warmth and light for them to fructify and grow. The period of her life of faith and duty had drawn to a close; but *even if she spoke in the tongues of men and of angels but had not love, or understood all mysteries and all knowledge, and had faith to remove mountains, she was nothing* (1Cor. 13:1). The story of Rhodesia's love had only been glimpsed in this book, yet it had been as vibrant and eventful as her missions, and when her sun rose again, this love would empower her.

Epilogue

Some people spent a lifetime to acquire a house they could call their own, whereas others had several grand houses they considered trophies for a fortune they built. For Rhodesia, houses were important for the events, memories and emotions they carry and symbolize. Somehow, the houses she had been through told the story of her life, her battles and glories, the loved ones she gained and lost, the wisdom she learned, and tangible evidence of endless blessings and support of an ever beneficent Creator.

Who knows where she would be placed in the next half of her life? There was a song that goes,

"We're on the road,

We move from place to place,

And oftentimes when I'm about to call it home,

We'd have to move along.

The friends we know,

We meet along the way

Too soon the times we share

Form part of yesterday."

The houses she had been through were never gone, because they, and the people that graced those houses stayed in her heart. All she knew was that wherever the wind took her, she would do good, make friends, love, learn, pray, trust, and radiate her ray of light.

About the Auhtor

Rhodesia

Rhodesia has written poetry since the tender age of three, was once hailed as Philippines' Youngest Author at the age of nine, having compiled an anthology of poems. Her writing craft paused when she focused on clinical, academic, and administrative duties as a physician. Currently a devoted mother of two, she has rejuvenated her love for the written word.

www.ingramcontent.com/pod-product-compliance
Lightning Source LLC
Chambersburg PA
CBHW021327160726
47994CB00004B/1655